Introduction

Desire- noun: A strong feeling of wanting to have something or wishing for something to happen.

Fantasy- noun: The faculty or activity of imagining things, especially things that are impossible or improbable.

For these individuals, Their fantasies and desires took over their dreams. It consumed their thoughts and made traditional sex boring and lackluster. See what happens when they decide to let their inhibitions go and try "Something New"...

You... Me... and She makes 3

For Christina and Thomas, life was routine and monotonous. Wake up, go to work, come home, catch up on their television programs and sleep. If they were lucky, one of them wouldn't pass out on the couch and they'd get a quick round of sex in. The foreplay was predictable, and the session usually lasted minutes.

But Christina was hiding a secret desire. She always seemed to find herself fantasizing about women. Well, one woman in particular. Her friend, and colleague Maritza. She was a gorgeous Latina with the perfect J-Lo body. She lived the life that Christina could only dream of. She was sexually liberated and would entertain her with stories of her late-night trysts with men and women alike. She spoke of achieving multiple orgasms that sent tingles down Christina's spine and made her throb with desire.

At the same time Thomas, who up until now was just happy he was able to snag a girlfriend who was willing to be his in-house sex partner, was enamored with the idea of a threesome· All of his friends had stories of their wild days of orgies and threesomes. Since he and Christina were high school sweethearts, he never got to experience any of those "wild days". The thought of having two sets of breasts to play with was very arousing for him.

One day, while Christina was drunk off of one too many glasses of wine, she decided to reveal her girl crush to Thomas. She was worried that he would get upset that she desired someone other than him. She couldn't have been more wrong! He was "legit down" with the whole idea and actually encouraged her to reach out to Maritza.

She decided to put it all out on the line and tell Maritza how she felt through text message. She always thought she picked up on a flirtatious vibe and she was full of liquid courage by the name of Chardonnay; chilled with a little slush in the glass. She let her know how much she admired her free spirit. That she thought she was absolutely gorgeous and fantasized about her often. She invited her over for a little wine and a lot of sex with her and Thomas. She read over the message, and before she lost her nerve; She hit "send". A feeling of sheer terror hit her in the bottom of her gut that made her feel she had swallowed cement. What if Maritza didn't like her that way and she rejected her advances? Or even worse, what if she reported her to Human Resources for sexual harassment. She was horrified and kicked herself for not thinking things through properly. Before Thomas could even think of what to say to console her, she heard a text alert from her iPhone.

It was Maritza. To her surprise, she shared how she was equally attracted to Christina. She said she always wanted to speak on it but didn't want to offend her. That was why she shared so many sexual experiences with her, hoping that she may one day get the hint. Maritza asked for the address and time that she should arrive. They put their plans in motion. Ready or not... This was really going to happen.

Thomas was shocked at how easy the whole process was. You usually only read about stuff like this in books; or watch it in some raunchy porn video, but this was real life. He was going to be able to act out his new found fantasy. But what made it even better was that it was all Christina's idea.

They straightened up and lit some candles. They cut on some soft music and chilled another bottle of wine from their collection. Christina decided to put on something sexy and silky for the occasion. Thomas decided to play it cool and wear some basketball shorts and a tank to show off all his hard work in the gym. Christina walked up to him and kissed him deeply. He could tell just how excited she was and it turned him all the way on. His shaft got rock hard and Christina felt it press up against her stomach. She smiled and grabbed it through his shorts.

"Save some of that excitement for when Maritza gets here," she said as she walked away to prepare a cheese and fruit platter. Christina wanted the ambiance of the place to be perfect for the occasion.

11:30 pm on the dot. Maritza texted Christina to let her know she was outside. Christina went to open the door, heart pounding so hard she thought it would jump out of her chest. She took a deep breath and opened the door. Standing there in a slinky black dress and 6-inch red pumps was Maritza. She looked especially gorgeous that night. Christina welcomed her inside and locked the door behind her. When she spun around to face Maritza, she was greeted with a warm soft kiss on the lips. It tasted of mint and berries and made her shiver from pleasure.

"I'm sorry, I've just been dying to do that ever since I met you," Maritza said after their lips parted ways. Christina blushed and assured her there was no need to be sorry and that the feeling was truly mutual. Thomas, who was peeking in from the bedroom decided he better go out there and introduce himself before they got started without him. He walked in and presented his hand to Maritza so she could shake it. She laughed and gave him a hug instead. "This isn't a business meeting Thomas, you don't have to be so formal," she said to him. Christina giggled as well because she could see just how nervous he actually was.

They decided to take the party to the couch and Christina poured 3 glasses of wine. She was still a little tipsy from the four cups she had earlier in the evening, but some of the effects wore off while she prepared for their evening together.

They sipped and ate the cheese and fruit. Christina and Maritza took turns feeding Thomas and he felt like King of the World. Before they knew it, Christina and Maritza were making out right in front of him: Christina to the left of him and Maritza to the right. He watched as their tongues intertwined and did a beautiful dance of passion. Since he was in the middle he decided he would feel them both up at the same time. He rubbed their thighs and massaged their breasts. He was so turned on by the whole situation and nothing really even transpired yet. Christina had perky B cup breasts that he loved to play with. They fit in his hands perfectly. Maritza, on the other hand, had large breasts, a D cup at the very least. They were going to take more than one hand to hold and he looked forward to the opportunity.

She must've read his mind because she slid the straps down and exposed her full bosom to him. Her nipples were a dark chocolate brown, and were larger in size. They looked so suckable, but he didn't want to jump the gun too soon.

He looked to Christina who seemed to read his mind and gave him an approving look to just have a good time. She slipped her straps down to her lingerie and exposed her pair with the pretty golden color nipples. She was half black and half Caucasian and her nipples were the perfect blend of both races.

He leaned in and began licking and sucking Christina's first. He was still being careful not to show too much attention to Maritza right away. To his surprise, Christina leaned over and started sucking on Maritza's chocolate-colored nipples. He decided to join in and took her other breast into his mouth. They sucked and licked her nipples as if she were as chocolate tasting as they looked. She let out a sexy moan that they both seem to feel.

The three of them began kissing each other. Tongues and lips were everywhere. They tasted of wine and felt so good. Both Maritza and Christina slipped off their clothes and began to undress Thomas together. The three of them stood naked and exposed in the middle of the living room.

They decided to take the party to the bedroom. Christina and Maritza climbed in bed together first and Thomas just stood there taking in the sight.

Both of them were so different. Christina was a beautiful caramel complexion with sandy brown hair that coiled up into a fro. She was tall and had legs for days. Her athletic body was complimented by her plump apple-bottom booty. She had green eyes with flecks of gold throughout them and the pinkest, softest lips he ever kissed.

Maritza was a tiny woman with a fair complexion. She had long straight black hair that reached the small of her back. She had dark brown eyes that looked like she was hiding a secret and nice full lips. Her little body held up those full breasts of hers and she had a nice tight round booty. Together, they were any man's perfect fantasy.

After taking in every inch of them he decided to join them in the bed. They all began kissing again and exploring their bodies with their hands. Christina kissed down Thomas' chest and licked all the way to his shaft. She took him into her mouth and slid all the way down slowly. His penis jumped in her mouth from both excitement and pleasure. She began giving him the best head she'd ever given him.

Up and down she went while gently stroking the base. Maritza inched herself to the edge of the bed and spread his legs slightly apart. She began licking his balls simultaneously with Christina's sucking. He had never experienced such an amazing sensation. Before he could get a handle of himself he exploded his sweet fluids all down Christina's throat. It was so unexpected, she didn't even have time to decide if she wanted to catch it. She was glad she swallowed it because it tasted like pineapples and it turned her on even more.

Next, Maritza decided to show Christina just how much she had been wanting her. She laid her back and spread her legs far apart. She dived deep into her pretty pink peach and began licking her pleasure zone. It was slightly fuzzy like a peach and just as sweet as one too. She licked and sucked up and down and all around. Christina felt waves of pleasure flow through her body. It was warm and electric. Thomas watched as the woman he loved made fuck faces and it was sexy as hell. He wanted to be inside her at that very moment but held back so she could continue enjoying herself. Maritza squeezes and rubbed on Christina's firm thighs as she feasted on her. Christina climaxed super hard and her body convulsed all over the bed.

Christina gained her composure and decided she wanted a taste of Maritza as well. She had never eaten another woman out before; just fingered one in college. She just did to her what she enjoyed having done on herself. She seemed to be doing an amazing job because Maritza was moaning and speaking in Spanish. "¡Por favor no pares Mami!" She said in the sexiest voice ever. It turned Christina on even more and it sent Thomas over the edge. As Christina ravished Maritza, Thomas went behind her and slid deep inside her. He slow-stroked her so that he wouldn't throw off her rhythm with Maritza. She was

dripping wet and the sounds it made was music to his

ears.

Maritza was so turned on by the sensations and the show

that was being put on in front of her. She orgasmed twice

back to back, both equally as strong. Now that Christina

was done lapping up Maritza's juices, it was fine for

Thomas to have his fun. He began pounding out Christina

from the back. He slapped her firm bottom and it jiggled

just enough to make him even harder. Christina squirted

all on his shaft and he put it into Maritza's mouth to suck

it all off. He then slid deep inside Maritza and she was wet

as hell. She was creamier than Christina and it made him

curious as to how she tasted. He didn't have to wonder for

long because Christina kissed him passionately, tasting

Maritza's flavor all on her tongue. She was sweet and a lot

different than Christina, but equally as delicious. This

made him speed up and pound out Maritza's pussy until she creamed all on his shaft. He pulled out and let Christina lick it off this time. He threw Christina's legs over his shoulders and banged her extra hard. He wanted her to be the one that got all of his love fluid. He poured out inside of her and collapsed on top of her chest. He was sweaty and out of breath. This was certainly more of a workout than their usual quick session.

He rolled off of Christina and laid between the two of them. Each of them cuddled up on his chest and stared at him; and then each other. They had opened up Pandora's box and loved what was inside. This may have been their first time, but it most certainly wouldn't be their last.

Marcus and Noelle... Voyeurism in the park

Noelle loved to live life on the edge. She enjoyed excitement and thrill-seeking. She was so glad to find Marcus who shared in her same interests. They hit it off immediately and were married within months of meeting. Despite all of their wild adventures, it was one thing they had both never really tried. They both fantasized about having sex outdoors. Not just a quickie in the park, they had both been there and done that. They wanted to put on a performance. Months had went past, but they never actually acted on it.

Now it was their one year anniversary. Despite what everyone else was saying, they were more in love now than they were when they got married. Marcus decided he would give her the gift of making her fantasy come true. He put everything in motion weeks prior and today was the day. He instructed Noelle to put on something sexy, and they rode off together.

They pulled up to an abandoned park. It had a chain on the fence but it wasn't locked. Marcus unhooked the chain, and they drove inside until they reached a parking lot. It was dusk but the moonlight was just bright enough where you could make out silhouettes. There, in the middle of the grassy field, was a king-sized bed. It had red silk sheets on it and looked soft and inviting. All around it were folding chairs as if he was expecting company. Marcus was so excited for the next phase of his plans. Just then, a group of masked individuals walked over and took their seats. They all had on sexy lingerie and pajamas. This was the moment he had been planning for; It was time for the show. Marcus grabbed Noelle by the hand and led her to the bed. He began undressing her slowly... teasing the crowd of silent onlookers. Noelle was nervous. All of these people were going to see her in her rawest form. She was slightly body-conscious but was even more turned on than afraid. Before she knew it she was completely undressed. The soft light from the moon cascading all over her body. He began to kiss her neck. Licking it just the way she liked it. Her nipples grew hard from the excitement. The chilly night air intensified the feeling and she felt them grow even harder. He took the left one into his mouth, sucking like he was famished and she was his nourishment. His tongue danced all around it. his lips kissed it so gently. It felt so good and she could feel herself getting moist from the sensation. He took the other one into his mouth and did the same thing. By this time Noelle was ready for whatever the night may bring. In the darkness, she could see the audience getting excited. Some were even rubbing on themselves and each other. This excited her even more. She grabbed Marcus by his belt buckle and began to loosen it. His manhood began to grow in anticipation. She pulled his pants and underwear down simultaneously, exposing all he had to offer. She slid him inside her mouth and began French-kissing the head. The cold air seemed to have no effect on him. He was fully erect and ready for action. She kissed and licked all around his penis and slowly slid all the way down. The men in the crowd began applauding and cheering her on. The women seemed to be studying her skills to put into practice later on. Marcus was moaning and shaking. Everything seemed intensified by the fact that they had an audience. She felt like she needed to show off even more. She laid him down and spread his legs. She began licking and sucking on his left testicle showing it the same attention he gave her nipple. He grabbed a handful of her hair and let out the sexiest groan ever. That only seemed to boost her performance and she got extra nasty with it. The left ball then the right one, and the seam in between. Her mouth was leaking and everything was sloppy wet. The strings of slobber looked like webbing between her fingers. It ran down under his balls and dripped into his crack. He had never had head like this from her or anyone else for that matter. He held on as long as he could but erupted in her mouth when she slid it back down her throat. She swallowed every drop and stuck her tongue out at the crowd so they could see. By this time a few were standing up out of their chairs and moving in closer for a better look. Before she could even decide if she was comfortable with it or not, she was flipped over on her back and had his face buried in her pussy. He devoured her feverishly, licking every inch of her. He threw her legs up in the air and pushed them towards her head. He licked her ass crack and slid his tongue in and out of her. She moaned loudly from the intense pleasure. This time the men were taking pointers and the females were mesmerized. He was equally good at oral copulation. He sent waves of euphoria through her body that curled her toes and made the hairs on the back of her neck stand up. Her nectar flowed from her right into his mouth and he was delighted to taste it. He bit her inner thigh and she just about lost all of her good sense. He was showing out too and the audience was elated. He took her legs and placed it over his shoulders. He slowly rose up until she was almost upside down. He slid deep inside of her and began slow-stroking her pussy. It felt agonizingly good as his rock-hard penis rubbed against her walls. She was made perfectly just for him. He hit her G spot and she responded with squirts of her nectar. Slap slap slap; everyone could hear the skin-to-skin interaction. A couple intensely watched while masturbating. It was creepy and erotic all at the same time. He flipped her over and wrapped his arm around to the front; choking her exactly the way she liked it. He slid in deep and pounded her hard and fast. He was unapologetic in his rhythm and it hurt so good. Noelle couldn't hold out any longer and she orgasmed multiple times. He was drenched in her juices and he loved every minute of it. She then pushed him back on the bed and decided to exact her revenge. She climbed on top of him and rode him like Seabiscuit, bouncing up and down and twirling her hips around. Every time she went down it felt like an ocean of fluids drenched his pole. She was so damn wet! She sounded creamy and her walls seemed to have suction. He came in less than 5 minutes and she tasted herself off of him, cleaning up the mess she had made. They got dressed and left the crowd of people to enjoy the bed. Most of them were in the act already. As they got in the car and pulled off, they laughed at what they had done. They agreed it was the most thrilling and frightening experience of their lives.

Cheryl's prison lover

Cheryl had terrible luck in men. They either cheated on her, used her for her money, or were a bit off in the head. She was so tired of meeting the same losers over and over in different form; so she had been single for a couple of years.

One day, while searching on google, she stumbled upon an ad for writeaprisoner.com. She had never considered talking to someone in jail, but she could definitely relate to feeling all alone. She clicked through the site and saw a picture of a man name Rio. He was tall, dark, and extremely handsome. He spoke of how he would be getting out later that year around Thanksgiving time and wanted to make a good friend that he could spend his holidays with. Something about him drew her in so deep and she knew she was destined to be in his life. She sent him a message and went on with the rest of her day.

The next day she went to check her email and saw she had a message from Rio. She wasn't expecting him to respond so quickly, but she was eager to see what he had to say. He thanked her for reaching out to him and complimented her on her good looks. She had attached a photo of herself in hopes that he would be pleased with what he saw. He indeed was.

He told her about his life and what landed him in that situation. He was eighteen and dumb and decided to rob the guy who shorted him when he sold him drugs. The guy only was short about forty dollars, but his reputation was on the line. He broke into his home and held him and his family at gunpoint. He collected his forty dollars and another two hundred for his troubles.

About a month later he got pulled over driving and found out he had a warrant for his arrest for the robbery. He learned that the woman went to the police and told them everything. She mentioned there were children in the house at the time, and that was the nail that sealed the coffin. He spent the last 12 years in prison paying for his dumb decisions.

They corresponded back and forth every day after that initial interaction. Dozens of emails and phone calls. She had fallen madly in love with him and the feelings were mutual. He was released just as he said, in the beginning of November, after completing all of his time. He was now free to be with her like they had dreamt about for so many months. They spent every day together trying to make up for the last 12 years he had missed in every way imaginable.

It was now Christmas day. Everything was prepared and Cheryl and Rio were in their apartment together. They decided to invite a few friends and family members over to celebrate. They stayed up all night preparing the feast for everyone. They prepared a roasted turkey with cornbread dressing. Honey baked ham with the pineapple rings just like mama used to make. Greens, macaroni and cheese, candied yams, deviled eggs, and a table full of desserts big enough to cure any sweet tooth. After staying up the whole night before cooking, it was time for Cheryl to get dressed before company arrived. She went upstairs and pick out a cute little outfit that was perfect for the festivities. She walked over to Rio and gave him a nice deep kiss for all of his help in the kitchen. He felt that kiss all the way down to his loins and it makes him grow in excitement. Since they'd been in their home living as a couple, it seemed as though they couldn't get enough of each other. Rio decided to make Cheryl's shower a little more enjoyable. He followed her to the bathroom and watched her take off all her clothes. She slid them off slow and sensual, trying to give Rio a little preview before the main attraction. By this time he was standing at full attention and couldn't wait to salute her. I finish undressing and put on some Jodeci's greatest hits. Cheryl lit their candles and cut off the bright lights. Their bathroom looked like the scene of a sexy music video. The room was filled with the smell of honey and melon. She stepped into the shower and let the water cascade down her body. The way the candlelight was flickering he could see glimpses of her body wet in the light. Rio quickly took off his boxers and came in to join her.

Rio was so excited and eager to be inside of her, but she told him to slow down and be patient. She wanted to make love to him; Not just have sex. Rio agreed and lathered up

Cheryl's body sponge. He began washing her back. They

cleaned each other from head to toe, paying extra close

attention to the body parts that made them shiver from

pleasure. Once they rinsed off Rio began kissing her neck

down to her back and then her butt cheeks. He spun her

around and placed one leg over her shoulder. He began

exploring her with his tongue, tasting her like he hadn't

eaten in weeks. It feels so good that Cheryl could hardly

keep her balance from her legs shaking. They decided to

take the party to the bedroom.

The room was already dark from the curtains they had

bought that blocked out the light. They brought in the

candles with them so they would have enough light to see

each other's cum faces. Plus, Rio loved the way Cheryl's

body looked and her fuck faces when he was deep inside of

her. He threw her down on the bed and began devouring

her. His tongue hit every pleasure spot. He knew her body and knew exactly what she liked. Cheryl began to feel a wave of pleasure that started at her inner thighs and ran through her body down to her toes. She moaned in ecstasy. Cheryl was loud but she didn't care. Nobody was around and right then, the only people who existed were She and Rio.

She had to gain her composure because it was her turn to show out. The Virgo in her would not be outdone. She made him lay down on his back and began to kiss his lips, tasting her sweet juices off of his tongue. He loved it when Cheryl kissed him right after he tasted her and it had him rock hard. She worked her way down from his neck to his chest. She licked the trail down Rio's stomach and ended up at the tip of his dick. She began kissing the head, licking and sucking all around the tip. She then slid him all the way into her mouth and down her throat. She had no gag reflexes so she did it with ease. Cheryl slowly came up, while tightening her mouth just enough for Rio to feel it grip his dick. Her mouth was warm, wet, and inviting. She slid up and down and licked all around. Faster then slower. Rio had his hand on the back of her head so he was guiding her pace. Cheryl wanted to do it exactly how he liked. Rio felt the pressure build up and let Cheryl know he was going to explode any second. She sped up in anticipation of his climax. His nut flowed all into her mouth as he shivered from pleasure. Cheryl swallowed every drop and kept going until he couldn't take anymore. One to one... they were now tied.

Rio was still very hard because he was so turned on by the way she sucked out every bit of what he had to offer. He threw her legs over his shoulders and slid deep inside her. She let out a gasp from the pleasure. He began stroking her slow and deep. In and out... in and out... She was getting wetter with every stroke. Rio looked at Cheryl in her eyes and enjoyed all the faces she was making. He began to suck and lick her nipples and he sped up inside her. She came all over his dick and her walls tightened up around him. Rio flipped her over and begin beating it up from the back. This time it was fast and hard. It was raw and animalistic. He had the rhythm of an African drum. Boom.. boom.. boom.. boom... The arch in her back was at the perfect angle. She was throwing it back at the perfect tempo. Her ass jiggled and he could see all the wetness every time he pulled out of her a little. Rio pulled Cheryl's hair and smacked her ass just the way she liked it. He tried to hold on a little longer but Cheryl tightened her muscles around him again and he poured out deep inside her. It felt so good that he collapsed right on top of her.

They were so out of breath that they just laid in the bed and stared at each other. It was completely silent except for the music playing in the background and their heavy breathing. Cheryl interrupted by saying "best shower ever" and they both burst out into laughter. They laid there a little while longer cuddling each other and talking about life's plans. They had waited so long to be able to have this very moment. Just the two of them, and the years they had ahead of them that they would spend together.

Natasha and Aaron... All tied up

Success came easily to Natasha. She did what she was
supposed to do and never deviated from the plan. She was
valedictorian all through school and graduated top five of
her college class. She went into marketing and got a high
paying job at a firm that represented multi-billion dollar
corporations.

She lived in a lavish brownstone in a posh area of
Manhattan all by herself. All the hard work she put into
her career made it impossible for her to make any real
romantic connections. She had a little Yorkie named

Snickerdoodle, and a fish named Nemo to keep her company. But, she longed for more of an adult connection. Total, she had only ever been with three men. Kenny from the neighborhood who took her virginity. Deshawn from that one time she drank too much at a college party. Finally, there was Terrance. The only serious relationship she ever had. It lasted all of 2 years and she thought they would get married. Too bad he ended up already having a wife. She popped up at Natasha's job after work and introduced herself with receipts of his transgressions. That catastrophe ended about 2 years ago and she was ready to get out there and explore.

During this hiatus from men, she got really into porn. She had purchased a few toys from her sister Shannon's sex line and decided she'd get to know herself. Throughout her exploration phase, she discovered she had an affinity for the "rougher" genres of porn. The force, the aggression, turned her the fuck on. She always wanted to be in charge, and to control the men around her. In her male-dominated field of work, coupled with the disaster that was her first and last serious relationship, she wanted to finally feel in charge.

She decided to look online one day one day for likeminded groups on Facebook. BDSM for beginners was where she decided was the best fit for her. Everyone was so friendly and forthcoming about their kinky fetishes. They showed instructional videos on different techniques, educated them on proper terminology, and posted the funniest memes. Everyone pretty much interacted with everyone, but there was one particular gentleman that was especially interested in Natasha. His name was Aaron. Last names have been asked to keep secret for the privacy of the parties involved.

Aaron flirted a lot with Natasha, and asked her to be his master. He was equally excited by the idea of being totally helpless and Natasha seemed like the perfect one to practice with. He would often send her inboxes of his desires with her. She started off being really sexually attracted to him, but it quickly evolved into more. They conversed every day on the phone and would video chat often. Sometimes the video sessions would get a little X rated, and she showed him all of her tricks with her toys. He made her feel so free to be herself. It was so amazing.

Finally, the time came for them to meet in person. They decided the first night he was in town, they would just have a traditional date. Dinner and a few cocktails while they made sure the chemistry was as real in person as it was over the phone. They made reservations at a quiet hip bistro on the south side of town. The booths were draped in red linen that made it super intimate. She wore a sexy burnt orange colored dress with a pair of nude pumps. She decided on a dainty gold necklace to accent her bronze skin and her sexy collar bone. Her hair was curled like a fifties pinup model. She oozed sex appeal.

She arrived first so that she could make herself more comfortable. She had to make sure they got the booth in the corner. Her job had her around some high profile people sometimes, and she seemed to have developed a paparazzi following of her own. She couldn't take the chance of them ruining her evening. She wanted complete privacy with him.

He arrived ten minutes early with a bouquet of flowers. He looked fine as hell. He had on a nice tailored shirt and jacket with dark wash denim jeans. He looked expensive and smelled like success. He waved and flashed a large gold Rolex on his wrist. He certainly wasn't afraid to show off his financial status. They ordered the raw oysters and some dirty martinis.

Throughout the night conversation went amazing. He was funny, intelligent, charismatic, and called her names like Goddess and Master all night. She felt so sexy and empowered. By the end of the date, she knew she was going to invite him over the next night.

It was a Friday night. Natasha had just gotten out of the shower and lotioned up her body with raw shea butter and organic coconut oil. She applied her makeup just right and put her hair in a high ponytail. She chose a blood red lipstick and dark smoky eye to match the occasion. She put on her leather corset and cinched her waist as tight as it could go. She slipped into her fishnet stockings; taking extra care not to rip them. She put on her little leather skirt that barely covered anything and her thigh high six-inch stiletto heel boots. She sprayed herself with Versace Bright crystal perfume. It was her absolute favorite.

After she looked in the mirror for a while, making sure she was pleased with what she saw, she headed to her special closet. She had assembled quite the collection thanks to lonely nights and online shopping. Natasha picked out a couple pairs of handcuffs, a small whip, and a cock-ring. She never used one before, but watched enough videos to know how to use it. She gathered everything into a basket and headed down to her basement that she set up as a sex dungeon. She laid out all her toys and finished setting everything up just right. This was going to be the first time she showed him her dominant side. They had talked about it all the time while discussing their fantasies, and tonight was the night they were going to act it all out.

As she put the finishing touches on everything , she heard the doorbell ring. She headed back upstairs and opened the door. There, standing in the doorway was Aaron: a beautiful bald caramel man· He took a long look at her up and down and she could tell he was very pleased with what he saw. He licked his lips and bit his bottom lip just the way she liked it. As sexy as he was, she couldn't break character. She grabbed him by his collar and lead him inside. She ordered him to follow her down to her dungeon. He was already growing in anticipation. He saw all the kinky things she had set up and knew it would be an amazing night. As Aaron began to speak to tell her how amazing she looked she gave him a quick slap to the face.

"Did I tell you to speak?" She said, in her most dominating voice. That turned him on and he immediately apologized to his master. They had discussed all the hard and soft limits and settled on the color system for their safe words. "Green" meant go; everything is great. Yellow is caution or slow down. I'm not comfortable or this hurts a little more than expected. Red means stop and they would be sure to honor the system. She knew the slapping was right up his alley.

Natasha decided to give Aaron a hug instead, and placed his hands right on her ass. He smelled her sweet perfume and his manhood pressed up against her. He squeezed her soft cheeks and she let out a slight moan. She sat him down in her riding chair and climbed right on top of him.

She licked his face and then kissed him aggressively in his mouth. Their tongues twisted around each other as if they were doing a forbidden dance. He reached up to grab her ass again, but she forced his hands back down to his side. "Did I say you could touch me?" She said as reached for her whip. She gave him 2 quick whacks and told him to apologize. His manhood was fully engorged with excitement. "Sorry Master," he said in a voice that sent waves down to her pearl and made it throb with delight. He was so fucking sexy; especially when he was turned on. She ripped a hole in the crotch or her stockings, laid the back of the riding chair flat, and sat right on his face. "Eat slave!" She said as she began to grind on his lips. She could feel the juices begin to flow out of her. He let out a deep "Mmm sound" and tasted her feverishly. He licked and slurped and sucked with precision. Every flick of the tongue felt like lightning. She rocked her hips faster and faster, moaning and biting her bottom lip. She tried to fight the inevitable, but she came all over his face. His chin hairs dripped with her juices. She got up and licked it right off. She kissed him again tasting his tongue and her flavor. Next, she ordered him to suck her toes. He was a true freak and had a foot fetish so he was more than happy to obey. He unzipped her boots and slid them off. He reached up her skirt and removed her stockings. He made sure to gently rub across her pussy lips as he did. She wanted to say fuck the role play and attack him right then and there but she maintained her composure. She took her foot and placed it on his chest. He had already assumed the position and was on his knees in a praying position. She gently but forcefully pushed into his chest with her foot, bringing him down to a sitting position. She ordered him to open his mouth and she slid her toes right in. He licked and sucked each toe with such care. She shivered from the sensation. It tickled but felt good at the same time. "That's a good boy," She said to him as he kept sucking away. He started rubbing his hands up her legs and she gave him a couple more thrashings of her whip. His manhood jumped from excitement! She ordered him to lay on the bed and she handcuffed his arms to the railing. She slid his pants off and slid her tongue across the head of his dick. She began French-kissing it and felt him grow in her mouth. It turned her on. She stopped and ordered him to beg for more. He didn't need to be told twice. He was so horny that just might explode, so he begged and begged until she was satisfied. She slid him all the way down her throat and just held him there. She could feel his dick pulsating in her throat and she knew he wouldn't last too much longer. She wasn't ready for him to cum yet. She slid him out and put the cock-ring on his dick. It was tight and had him harder than he'd ever been. She opened his legs and began licking his balls. Left, then right, then both of them together. She licked that line that goes down the sack and divides the scrotum. He shivered and let out a "fuck!" Instantly her juices started running down her thighs. She lifted the sack and licked the taint; that space between the balls and the butt. Aaron was moaning about as loud as she was when he was sucking her pussy. She twirled her tongue and flicked it with such intent. She then lifted his legs and before he could protest, she was licking his ass crack and hole. He was squirming and moaning louder than she ever heard before. He liked that a lot! She took some of the slobber that had run down his dick and began to stroke his manhood as she ate his "groceries". He didn't care. His legs were in the air and his ass was being licked and he didn't give a single fuck! It felt way too good to care. She removed the cock ring and made her way back up to his shaft. She wanted to taste his cum. She began sucking fast and sloppy. Her slurping noises were loud and his whole body began convulsing. He erupted like a fire hydrant in her mouth. She just kept going and he felt his soul leave his body. Jill Scott didn't have shit on her! She swallowed and swallowed until she had consumed everything he had to give. As much as he has just come, she was sure he would need a break. To her surprise, his dick never lost an inch and it was just as hard as it was before he came. She was impressed. She stood up, removed her tiny skirt, and turned her back to face him. She placed a foot on each side of his body and slid down on his pole like a firefighter. She bounced up and down and swirled her hips. He felt so good inside of her. Her juices were dripping everywhere .

Aaron moaned as he watched her fat ass jiggling on his dick. She was riding him so well, and he was worried that he'd bust before she even had a chance to get herself off. Before he could even gather his thoughts she spun around on his dick and began riding him from the front. She never even let the dick slide out. She was good as hell. He felt as if he were

fucking a professional. She wrapped her hands around his neck and choked him as she rode him. He loved erotic asphyxiation and she was fulfilling his fantasy. She bounced faster and faster. Slapping him one minute and kissing him the next. Her perky breasts were going up and down and she had the look of a sex goddess on her face. He couldn't hold on any longer. Luckily for him, neither could she. She orgasmed over and over again. She squirted all over his dick and he burst deep inside of her. She collapsed on top of him and laid her head on his chest. It was like their heartbeats had synced up and played one melody. She took the keys to the handcuffs and freed her slave. She kissed him deeply and rested her head back on his chest. The whole night was "Super Green". There wasn't anything she did that he didn't like. This one would definitely go down in the books as one of the wildest play sessions ever.

She Kissed a Girl... and She Liked it

"I think you can never go wrong with a little black dress," Ebony said to Tyrell as she had him zip up her back. She was getting all gussied up for their "girl's" night out. She decided on her Gucci lace mini dress and some pumps. She put on a few bangles and some enticing perfume. She couldn't help but keep staring at her ring finger. Although Ebony had only been engaged a short while, there was a tan line from where the band used to be. Courtesy of the California sunshine. She shook the thought out of her head and replaced It with ones of turning up. She was going to have fun tonight even if it killed her.

Ebony threw back a double of Hennessy on her way out the door. She needed all the liquid courage she could get. They ordered a car for the evening. They had every intention of being too drunk too walk, let alone drive. Ebony and Tyrell hopped in the back like some celebrities. Tyrell had to be the one to spot the champagne in the cooler. "Time to drink and drown away our sorrows, it's what Beyoncé would want," he said jokingly, but with a slight hint of honest belief. She swore if they had to make a list of importance, it would go; The Father, the Son, the Holy Ghost, and directly under that was Beyoncé.

They poured a few glasses while listening to the lemonade album. They were going to be tipsy and ready to get in formation. As they pulled up to the LGBTQ bar Ebony felt confident. Either the champagne and Hennessy worked, or she was just ready to have a great time. She reapplied her lip gloss. The driver got out and opened the door. Tyrell stepped out first, then grabbed Ebony's hand and helped her out the car. They checked each over to make sure they looked their best: Perfection. They popped a stick of gum and headed inside.

The Vibe was the most popular LGBTQ bar in Los Angeles. Only The Who's who of the community could get in. Luckily Tyrell was so well known in the community, plus it didn't hurt that Ebony trained a few successful

LGBTQ individuals as well. They walked right in like they

owned the place.

"Boom boom boom boom", the music was thumping.

They walked in and landed right In the middle of a voguing

competition and it was heated. There were people cheering

for each side like the NBA finals. Ebony instantly felt

happier. Tyrell pulled her hand over to the bar. It was time

to refill their courage tanks, plus they needed to find a good

seat to "people watch".

"2 Hennessy and apple juices," he ordered. "Don't forget

our mineral waters with lemon," Ebony added, trying to

make sure they stayed hydrated. They sat and watched the

show as they waited on their drinks. They were " twirling

and death dropping" all over the place. Ebony was living for

this show. A few minutes later, the bartender interrupted

their gaze by handing them their drinks. Ebony reached In

her clutch to pull out her card when the bartender stopped

her. "No need, the young lady over there took care of it for you." He said as he pointed to the VIP section. Sitting there was a beautiful caramel woman with curly hair pulled into a bun. She dressed gender-fluid and was drop dead gorgeous. She waived over to them as to say, "please accept my gift."

Ebony blushed and raised her glass in her direction. "Ooooh bitch we been here all of 15 minutes and you already getting some play," Tyrell teased as he took a sip of his drink. Ebony was flattered and nervous at the same time. She had never been hit on by a woman in such a forward manner. They lived in California so of course, She got the feeling about certain people even flirted a time or two herself, but this was more up front and in her face. Besides kissing in college, she had never even been with a woman.

Ebony drank her drink quickly and washed it down with the mineral water. It felt like a warm hug going down, and that was just the comfort she needed.

All night long the sexy lady had been sending them free drinks. By this time Ebony had all the liquid courage she needed. They decided to go over there and thank her personally for her generosity. They stumbled a bit to her section but gained their composure before she could notice. She was taller than she looked from across the room. Even in her heels Ebony and the mystery woman looked eye to eye. All Ebony could think about was: "damn her eyes were beautiful." It was a shade of gray that reminded her of a cold winter's night. Her skin was smooth and her lips were full. She was attractive even to the straightest woman, and tonight Ebony definitely put the Q in LGBTQ. She spoke in a raspy, sensual voice.

"Hey beautiful, I was wondering what it was going to take to meet your acquaintance. I was going to send the whole bottle next," she said in a joking manner. Ebony giggled, then caught herself. She was giggling the way she would when she wanted someone to want her. Ebony managed to pull It together to say, "well thank you, beautiful, I enjoyed all the attention."

Ebony could've kicked herself because She did not know if she Identified as beautiful or not· She just smiled, and said,

"Beautiful huh? I'll take it," she grabbed Ebony by her waist and pulled her closer. She wrapped her arms around Ebony and gave her a long, deep hug. She was liquid in her arms and in her panties. It was a little pink g-string so she felt the moisture between her legs.

She let go and said, "My name is Jade. Jade Reed. I work for a PR firm here In LA."

Ebony looked over at Tyrell who was looking as If he was watching a television show unfold. He was absolutely no help. Ebony straightened her dress out and Introduced herself to her. Whatever this was between them was magnetic. Ebony was so drawn to her that she felt herself being pulled closer. She decided she needed to go freshen up and gain her composure. She excused herself to the bathroom and asked Tyrell to hold her drink. Ebony gave him this look to signal him that she needed him to break the tension while she was gone. She walked to the bathroom and grabbed some wet wipes off of the counter.

Ebony wiped her excitement from between her legs and sprayed a little perfume on herself. She splashed a little water on her face, hoping it would sober her up, or whatever it would take to stop wanting Jade the way her body did. Just then, She heard the door open up. It was Jade. She checked the other stalls and then locked the door behind her. She walked up to Ebony and grabbed her by her waist again. All of Ebony's effort to clean herself up went to waste. She was throbbing and dripping just from her embrace. She said,

"Don't fight it. I feel It too". Before Ebony could speak, she kissed her. She grabbed Ebony tighter and parted her lips with her tongue. Her lips were so soft. Her tongue tasted of liquor and pineapple juice. It was delicious. She felt Ebony's body give In to her. Every inch of her longed to be exactly where she was: in Jade's arms. She moved over to Ebony's neck and licked and nibbled it. It hurt so good. She took one of the straps to her dress down. She cupped Ebony's breasts and brought it to her mouth. She sucked and licked on them like she knew her body and knew exactly how she liked to be pleased. She lifted Ebony up on the counter and slid her finger up her dress. Part of her wanted to tell her no, but the other part was much stronger. Ebony felt her hand grabbing her thighs that were already drenched from wanting her. Jade stopped for a second and laughed.

"Oh she's ready for me huh," she said as she pulled Ebony's panties out the way. She took her finger and slipped it deep inside her wetness.

Ebony let out a moan that she hadn't heard in some time. It was the one that came out when she first made love to ex boyfriend Terrance. She realized she hadn't thought about him ever since she saw Jade's face.

Jade stroked Ebony in and out with her fingers. Deeper and deeper she went. Ebony thought she would scream from the pleasure.

Just when Ebony thought she'd explode she lifted her legs up in the air and dove in face first. She licked her clit with such precision. She continued to stroke her as she licked her pussy. It was some type of rhythmic pattern of ecstasy. She moaned as she ate as if she couldn't get enough of her. That sent Ebony over the edge. Her body convulsed in waves of euphoria. She felt as if she were floating away from her body. As she came to, Jade stood up and scooted closer between her legs. She kissed Ebony and told her she wanted her to taste how delicious she was. It was sweet, and warm, and wet. It was the best kiss Ebony ever had. Jade helped Ebony down off the counter and just smiled at her.

"Thanks for returning the drinks," she said as she grabbed Ebony by the hand and led her out the bathroom. She was hers. Jade had awakened something In Ebony that had been sleeping this whole time. She was ready to try something new.

They went back to the section and Jade sat Ebony right next to her. Tyrell seemed as if he knew exactly what had transpired. He handed Ebony her drink and told her he was going to go get his groove back too. He made his way over to one of his boy toys Ebony had met before. Jade rubbed her thigh and asked her if she needed anything else to drink. Ebony replied with, "another Hennessy and mineral water". Jade shot a sign to the mixologist and they made the drinks right up. She was having Ciroc and pineapple juice. She took a sip and smiled at Ebony. "Now you're going to owe me another drink too," she said with a sexy smile. The way she said it sent chills up Ebony's body. Jade wanted her to drink as much as she wanted. They spent the rest of the evening with each other. Tyrell left with his boo and Jade took the car back with Ebony.

They went back to Jade's condo that was right on the beach. They went out on the balcony and she made love to Ebony until the sun came up. She barely came up for air. She didn't want Ebony to please her, she just wanted her to lie back and take it. Ebony took it all in. Jade drank it all out. It was the best night they ever had.

Saying goodbye to our virginity

Desmond and Veronica grew up in the church. Monday choir practice. Tuesday member's meeting. Wednesday Bible study. Thursday's volunteering in the church's soup kitchen. Friday another choir practice. Saturday they got the day off and in church ALL day Sunday. They didn't mind, because there love for the Lord was so strong.

They attended the same Baptist church all throughout their lives and grew to be close friends. Since their parents were best friends, they often would see each other outside of church too. There was always talk that they were destined to be together one day. It couldn't have been truer.

When the two became teenagers, they attended a purity ball together. They, alongside the other teens of the church, made a commitment before God, the pastor, and their families; that they would save themselves for marriage. They planned on keeping that promise no matter what.

Seven years later and their promises were still being honored. As predicted; They had indeed fallen madly in love and were engaged to be married. They had made it to their 20th birthdays as virgins, and couldn't wait to say their vows and become husband and wife. They were especially looking forward to the wedding night.

For Desmond and Veronica, the pledge to abstain until marriage was a difficult one. They were so attracted to everything about each other, and everything made them filled with desire. They tried to pray it away together, but usually ended up making it to second base anytime they were around each other.

One time especially, they had been making out and they ended up inside of each other's pants. Desmond's penis was so long and hard in Veronica's hand. It was the first time she had ever seen or felt one in person and she was impressed.

Desmond was equally pleased with what he felt when he slid his fingers inside of Veronica. It was so warm and super wet. He had watched a few adult videos in his 30 years, but the clips did it no justice. It took everything in their power not to give in right then and there. They achieved their climax by rubbing on each other and spent the rest of the week repenting for it. They had several other close calls but managed to never go all the way.

The time had come. It was their wedding night. Their ceremony was beautiful and intimate. It took place in the church that had been so pivotal in creating their union. It seemed only fitting to say, "I do," where it all started. They had a nice dinner party instead of a reception. It was an easier decision than trying to figure out what they could and couldn't do in front of church members. They booked the honeymoon suite in the nicest hotel in town and had it decorated for the special occasion.

Desmond lifted Veronica in the air and carried her over the threshold in true traditional fashion. She was the happiest she'd ever been. They were finally husband and wife. she wrapped her arms around him and gave him the most passionate kiss she'd ever felt. It sent waves through her body and made her tingle in her panties.

Desmond brought Veronica over to their California king-size bed and laid her down gently. He leaned in and gave her another quick peck and said "hello Mrs. Steven," with the biggest grin on his face. She blushed and replied, "Hello Mr. Stevens." They were mutually ecstatic.

She laid there for a second, staring up at the ceiling and soaked it all in. In that very moment, she went from the responsible daughter to a grown woman. Someone's wife.

Her thoughts were interrupted by the sound of the jacuzzi being turned on.

"Come on in, the water's fine," said Desmond, already in his boxers, and waiting for the jacuzzi to fill. Veronica laughed and stripped off her wedding gown and waist cincher. She left on her lace white bra and thong. She was a chocolate-toned, six-foot tall Amazonian woman. She had a curly from that touched the clouds and could have been a model if she wasn't so unsure of her own beauty.

She walked over to Desmond and grabbed him right by his penis. He was already erect just from seeing her come across the room. She was truly the most beautiful girl he ever saw. Desmond was a handsome six foot seven, fair skinned man. He kind of looked like Ghost from the show Power or Omari Hardwick for the unhip. He could've had any woman he wanted, but he only had eyes for Veronica. They were fated to be together.

He felt a warm creeping sensation. Like the blood was hot lava, making its way up his penis so he could eventually erupt. It felt so good and he knew he had to calm down a bit or else he wouldn't last but mere seconds inside her.

Luckily for him, the jacuzzi was filled enough by now and he cut the jets on. He stepped down inside the tub and sat down slowly. The water was hot and it felt like he was literally tea-bagging the water. Veronica climbed in and joined him. She loved how hot and steamy the water was. It put her in a sexy mood like the scene out of a movie she knew she shouldn't be watching, but this time she was making her own.

She scooted up to him and got between his legs. She grabbed what was now rightfully hers and honorable in the eyes of God. she wasn't going to be shy about what she desired anymore. She stroked him up and down in the warm swirling water and he was ready to burst already.

He grabbed her by the hand and asked her to please wait. He explained how he wanted to enjoy more than her hand but she was making it very difficult. She giggled but understood. She let go and wrapped her arms around his waist. She pressed herself into him and licked his bottom lip. She followed with a gentle nibble and replied, "So what are you waiting for my love? Make love to me".

He was so damn turned on. He grabbed her forcefully by her waist and began kissing her passionately. Their tongues so intertwined they may never come undone. He unhooked her bra and threw it across the room. He wasn't going to act shy anymore with his desires either and right now he craved to have her in every way possible. He cupped her perfectly round C-cup breasts and began licking and sucking her dark chocolate nipples. They were full and perfect in size. First the right, then the left. She tasted so good and he was only more excited to be able to do as much as he wanted to with her.

He then slid hip pointer finger down her thong and grabbed it by the strappy waistband. He slid them all the way down her legs, going under the water, and threw it across the room where he had discarded her bra earlier· He slowly took his pointer and middle finger and rubbed up and down her clitoris. Stroking it up and down and mixing it with circular motions· For a virgin, he sure hit all the right spots. She licked her lips and moaned.. She felt herself getting ready to climax, and right before she could reach full peak he just stopped.

"You're not getting off that easy baby. I want all of you" He said and with that, he picked her up in the air and wrapped her legs around him. He slowly got out the jacuzzi and carried Veronica over to the bed. The whole time they never broke their gaze from each other. It was finally time to consummate their union.

He laid her down and stayed right on top of her. He kissed her neck down to her beautiful breasts and made his way slowly down to her lips. He kissed and licked all over and around them. Moving agonizingly slow but it felt so good. He licked and hit her inner thighs and it sent her over the edge. As soon as he placed the tip of his tongue onto her clitoris and licked it gently she squirted all over him. She shook and locked up from the euphoric sensation. He came up and kissed her on the lips, letting her taste just how sweet she really was. It was delicious.

She made him lay back and grabbed his penis and kissed the head. Licking in a circular motion and getting it nice and wet. He moaned and closed his eyes in pleasure. She began slowly going up and down his pole, teasing him the same way he teased her. He grabbed a fistful of her hair and his toes curled up with each motion.

He guided her head up and down but letting her control the speed. He wanted her to take her time with him. He enjoyed the build up. It was only intensifying his desire for her and solidified that he was going to rock her world. Or at least give it his very best efforts. She stopped sucking after she felt his penis growing harder and harder and told him she was ready.

He laid her on her back and slightly lifted her legs. He poked around a little but quickly found her opening. He slid inside her slowly, paying close attention to her pain level. Every video they ever watched and every person they've ever asked all told them how it's not pleasurable the first time for women.

For Veronica, that couldn't be further from the truth. She was ready. Even the pain of him " popping her cherry" was pleasurable. It stung and excited her all at the same time. It was done. She was no longer a girl, but a grown woman, a WIFE. Time to live out her adult fantasies and stop dreaming about them.

She told him to go deeper and he knew she was into it. He relaxed into his rhythm and sped up his pace. He lifted her long legs higher and placed them on his shoulders. He began to deep stroke her while sucking on her nipples. He was doing fine until she did something with the muscles of her vagina. It tightened up and locked down on him as if it were squeezing the toothpaste from the bottom of the tube and worked its way to the top. His nectar sprayed out more like a fire hydrant. He filled her insides up. They laid there, out of breath and on cloud nine. He was almost convinced they'd be leaving the honeymoon with a bun in the oven.

He didn't care. He couldn't wait to have kids with her. He couldn't wait to do everything with her. They were finally together and this was a forever kind of love.

Keep it Down, They'll Hear You

Nicole was such a goodie two-shoes. Always doing exactly what was expected of her and never deviated from the plan. She decided early on that she wanted to make the world a better place, so she got into volunteering. She traveled the world, bringing fresh water to remote villages and impoverished townships. She loved the life she lived.

The only thing she was missing was someone to share it with. She had never even had a real boyfriend before. Her focus had been solely on her work so she had no time for dating. How are you going to develop a connection when you never even know what country you are going to be in from month to month?

One day, while planning her next mission with the other people from her nonprofit organization, a handsome young man walked in. She had never seen him before because she would certainly remember him. He was tall, dark, with long dreadlocks. They were neat and twisted into barrels. He had a full manicured beard and the most interesting eyes. They were a regular shade of dark brown but they looked like they hid a lot of stories. She instantly felt a connection to him.

Peter, one of her fellow colleagues, stood up and approached the mystery man.

"Hey Bilal, I'm so glad you could make it." They exchanged a hug like they had been friends for years. Nicole thought to herself that Bilal was such a sexy name and suited him perfectly.

Her thoughts were interrupted by Peter introducing his friend to the group. "Everyone, I'd like to introduce you to my frat brother Bilal. We played basketball together until he decided to run off to Africa. He was one of the brainchildren that put together Project Rain."

Sexy and smart, Nicole was impressed. Project rain went to different villages and taught people how to properly collect and clean rainwater. They provided the tanks to the water to go in and the basic supplies needed to purify the water.

Thanks to the mission hundreds of people in Africa had clean drinking water.

Bilal walked up to everyone individually and shook their hands. She eagerly awaited her opportunity to meet his acquaintance. It was like he was saving her for last. She hoped her hands weren't too sweaty, because she was nervous as hell.

"Hello Queen, my name is Bilal. Nice to meet you," he said in a low sexy baritone voice that made Nicole tingle in her happy place. He gave her this look and all she could see is sex in his eyes. She felt as if he undressed her with his mind, and she hoped he'd get the opportunity to do it in real life.

Bilal took a seat and Nicole decided to play it cool. They were there to help the world; helping herself would have to come later. They planned a mission to Zimbabwe. There was a tribe there that desperately needed their help. They would combine Project Rain with their other services and turn the community around.

The following Thursday they took flight. It was a long 14-hour flight to reach their destination. Nicole boarded the plane and looked for her seat. Low and behold Bilal was sitting by the window in her row.

She felt her heart skip a beat and her hands clam up with sweat. Something about that man just turned her on. He looked equally pleased to see her and offered to let her sit by the window instead. Seeing as though it was her favorite seat on the plane, she graciously took his offer. They buckled their seatbelts and prepared for takeoff.

Up up and away they went. The announcement came on that they could remove their seatbelts and get comfortable for the long flight ahead. Nicole put her gel neck pillow around her and covered up with a blanket. It was only four in the morning and she figured she'd sleep the ride away. Bilal pulled out the 48 laws of power and began reading it. It was another plus that they had the same taste in literature. Nicole began to quote a passage out of the book and it made Bilal smile. He looked genuinely impressed.

Before they knew it, they had been talking for hours about everything under the sun. He was so well-rounded and cultured. He spoke of missions all around the world and all his hopes for the future. They had so much in common and their chemistry was magnetic.

The plane was a little cool in temperature and Nicole could see Bilal was cold. He had been shivering and his teeth actually chattered a time or two. She decided to offer him some of her blanket that she had been wrapped in throughout the flight.

He agreed to take some of the blanket and to her surprise, he snuggled up next to her.

She could feel the warmth from his skin on hers. It was as though a fire ignited between them. She took her hand and placed it on top of his. He smiled at her advances. He took his hand and placed it on her thigh. He began rubbing it up and down in slow sensual motion.

She had on a velour sweatsuit, so it felt like velvet as he caressed her thigh. She felt herself get moist from the sensation. She took his hand and placed it inside her pants so he could feel what his touch made her body do. He was taken aback but was more than willing to feel her juices.

He slid one of his long, thick fingers inside her lips and went straight for her clit. He rubbed it in a circular motion, moving with such precision. Nicole let out a moan that was louder than she expected it to be.

"Quiet down, they will hear you," he said with a sexy smirk on his face. He began to speed up the rhythm of his rubbing. Faster and faster he rubbed. Wetter and wetter she became. She exploded from all of the pleasure and shivered with euphoria. He slid his fingers out her pants and licked them right in front of her.

"You taste even better than you feel," he said, sucking all the juices off. Nicole gathered her composure and responded with,

"you haven't felt anything yet". She stood up in her seat and excused herself to the bathroom. As she scooted past Bilal she whispered in his ear to meet her in five minutes. She rubbed his crotch area and felt his long hard desire for her.

She switched her hips down the aisle and knew he never broke his gaze from her. She splashed some cold water on her face and dried her sweaty hands. She couldn't believe she let him touch her like that. Something about him made her feel she almost didn't have a choice in the matter. She wanted him on a whole other level and she could tell the feelings were mutual.

Her thoughts were interrupted by a tap on the door. She adjusted her clothing and opened it up. Standing there, was Bilal who looked more than eager to come inside.

It was a tight fit. He was a tall ripped man and that bathroom was barely big enough for Nicole's small frame. It didn't seem to bother him though and he took down her pants with one swift motion. He lifted her up and sat her on the back of the toilet. Placing her hoodie down first so she didn't sit right on the toilet. He lifted her legs straight up in the air and spread them far apart.

Bilal dove in head first and began licking her lips. Or kissed and caressed every inch of her, eating all she had to offer. She came within moments of his first lick. He was damn good.

She then pulled out his huge pole and placed it in her mouth. His eyes rolled back and he let out a long "S" sound like a snake. She knew she had him where she wanted him. She moved up and down while twirling her tongue all around. Her mouth was dripping all down his penis. He grabbed the back of her head and began to shake. Warm sweet juices poured from him and it tasted so good.

He then lifted her in the air and slid deep inside her. He banged her like a drum and he could hear how much she loved every minute of it. She came one after the other after the other. Each time just as hard as the last. He kissed her deeply while she wrapped her legs around his waist and held on for the ride of her life.

He whispered in her ear that he wasn't pulling out and she agreed with him. He poured out inside of her and left his pole inside of her even after he was done. Her heart was racing and her breath was shaky. She never wanted to break their embrace.

After they caught their breath, they cleaned themselves up. Nicole slid out the bathroom first and walked back to her seat. It was as if the whole plane knew what she had done and all eyes were on her. Five minutes later Bilal walked back and sat next to her. He agreed that they must've been louder than they thought because all eyes were on him too. He admitted he never did anything like that before and was happy he joined the mile high club with her.

Nicole was just as new to the club as Bilal and was happy that she experienced it with him as well. He snuggled back under the covers with her and kissed her on her cheek. He leaned in and whispered "Just so you know, you're mine now," in her ear. It made her throb all over again and she let him know the feelings were mutual.

She may have stepped on that plane single, but she would land in Africa with her new man in tote, ready to take on the world... together.

FaceTime Fucking

Erica and Daniel had a healthy sex life. They loved to do it, and they loved to do it often. They even would schedule their lunch at the same time so they could meet up and have sex at least twice a week. The only thing they had more in common than their libido was their work ethic. Daniel owned a multi-billion dollar tech company and Erica was the CEO of global operations. She was the one taking the trips all over the world and landing deals with other prestigious companies.

They loved what they did, but it was starting to take a toll on their love life. Erica, who was always at work, found herself staying later to meet deadlines and close deals.

Since Daniel owned everything, he had more leisure time to do what he wanted.

One day, after a successful conference call, Erica went back to her office. She looked at her schedule for the rest of the day, another long night was ahead of her.

Suddenly her phone rang, interrupting her sulking. It was Daniel. Even after all their years together, she still got butterflies whenever his picture came across her phone.

"Hi babe, how's the best CEO in the world doing today?" He asked smiling at her lovingly. He had FaceTimed her from in the bathtub. His body was glistening from the water. He looked damn good.

"My day is great especially now that I get to talk to you," Erica responded. She Unbuttoned her top button to expose a little cleavage. She let her hair down out of the neat bun and shook it free. She knew it turned Daniel on to see her let loose. Some naughty secretary fantasy he had conjured up when they first started talking.

"Now baby you know what that does to me," he said as he lowered the camera down to his waist. Displaying the erection he had saluting from the water.

It was beautiful. Erica instantly got moist from the sight of it. "Can Ms. Twila come out to play?" He asked as he began stroking his pole from the bottom to the tip. Ms. Twila was the name Erica gave her vagina years ago. She talked about it joking with him one day, and He'd been calling it that ever since.

"Daniel, you know I'm working. I have a full day ahead of me and can't be masturbating in my office." She knew she was going to do it anyways, but she just loved hearing him beg for it. So damn sexy. He began stroking a little faster and moaning in a deep sensual tone. Her pussy throbbed at the sound of him. She got up, locked the office door, closed the blinds, and told her assistant she would be taking lunch.

Erica then opened her blouse completely and unhooked her bra, exposing her hard nipples. She began rubbing them and biting her bottom lip. "You like this daddy?" She said in my come-hither voice.

"Yes I love it!" he said in a breathy, aroused voice. She could tell he was getting close to climaxing. She pulled up her skirt, pulled down her lace white panties, and spread her legs wide open. She started rubbing Ms. Twila,

moaning from the pleasure.

"Damn baby I wish you were inside me right now!" She said, rubbing herself in a quick, circular motion. He could hear just how wet she was and it was dripping.

He was beating it super fast now. The veins in it fully

engorged with blood. He was rock hard. It drove Erica

crazy. Just then, his fluids shot out everywhere. It dripped

down his shaft into his curly brown pubic hairs. Erica felt a

tingle that started from her head and rushed over her

entire body. She held back her moans the best she could,

but still made more noise than she felt comfortable making.

Daniel started laughing and said,

"Hopefully the walls are soundproof," Erica felt instantly

embarrassed but enjoyed every bit of it. She couldn't wait

to get back home to make him pay for influencing her to

act out like that at work. She hoped he was ready because

Ms. Twila was not going to hold back.

Check out Trade

Christopher was a gay black man. From the time he was a little boy, you'd see him playing barbies with his sisters instead of outside roughhousing with the neighborhood boys· He even tried dating a few girls before he came to terms with his sexuality.

The day he came out, it was more of a sigh of relief to

everyone instead of a shock. Everyone was just happy he

could be his authentic self. He had the support of his loved

ones.

He spent his high school years in band and studying so he

could make it out of his small town. He wanted to explore

the world and find a place where he felt freer to be his

authentic self. When the time came to pick a college, he

settled on Clark University in Atlanta, Georgia.

All of his gay friends from school were going to be going

there plus it was a very LGBT-friendly city. He settled on

studying political science and fit in effortlessly.

One day, while grabbing an iced coffee before class, he saw

a gorgeous chocolate man. He had on a football uniform

that showed off his solid thick physique and it made

Christopher want to tackle him. He went out of his way to

walk past him so he could get a better look. To his surprise, the manly melanated God actually spoke to him. "Good morning, what do you suggest I get from here? I'm new to this whole coffee thing, but stayed up all night finishing my paper."

Christopher, who was giddy as could be, decided to play it cool and told him to get a Carmel frappe with an extra shot of espresso.

"Thanks a lot, man you're a lifesaver. My name is Calvin by the way. Nice to meet you," He shook Christopher's hand with a death grip. He could only imagine what else he could do with his hands.

"I'm Chris," he said trying to shake his hand equally as strong. He knew he looked gay from a country mile away but didn't want to scare off his manly new acquaintance.

He decided to play it cool until he could pick up more vibes from him.

"Well, I'm living in the Q frat house. Hopefully, I'll see you around sometime," Calvin said and gave Christopher a look that oozed sex. He walked out and Christopher enjoyed the view from behind.

Later that evening, Christopher decided to tell his roommate about his new crush. His roommate was in his third year there and was just as gay as he was. He knew everyone on campus and would surely know exactly who Chris was talking about.

Sure enough, he did. He explained to Chris that he had a whole girlfriend, but picked up on his "trade" behavior a time or two before. He lived a straight life, but something about him definitely gave off a gay vibe. Christopher decided he'd attend the Q's frat part that upcoming Friday to figure it out for sure.

Christopher felt like a stalker. He'd gone back to that coffee house every day that week hoping to run into Calvin again. He must've been telling the truth about not drinking coffee, however, because he never returned. It was now Friday and he wouldn't have to wait to see his crush any longer.

He picked out his favorite pair of skinny jeans and a nice button down shirt. He threw on his gold watch and chain. He put on a pair of dressy boots and some Creed cologne. His roommate put on some hot pink shorts and a black muscle shirt. He dressed flamboyantly as ever but had the respect of the whole campus.

They made their way to the Q's frat house and went right inside. The place was packeting true Greek status. Hip hop music was thumping from the speakers, and there was an ocean of red solo cups everywhere. Chris grabbed a Corona and started looking around for his boo (or at least in his head he was).

Just when he thought that maybe Calvin wasn't there, he saw him snuggled up in the corner with a petite redbone woman. She was beautiful, definitely the Barbie to his Ken. They seemed legitimately interested in each other and Christopher felt heartbroken. He knew he had a girlfriend, but couldn't help but feel that they had a connection.

He decided to suck it up and go speak to Calvin. He walked up and shook his hand again. Calvin introduced Chris to his girlfriend Delilah and told him he was glad he could make it. The whole time Calvin's gaze burned a hole into Christopher's soul. That look was the same look he gave him at the coffee house and he knew it couldn't be just his imagination. He decided to play it cool once again and wait until he got Calvin alone. He would simply just ask him how he felt. No use in beating around the bush any longer.

Christopher went on about the rest of his night with his roommate. They drank, ate, and vogued the house down. If Calvin didn't know he was gay before that party he certainly knew it now. Chris was twerking and working his body. Every once in a while he would catch Calvin staring at his moves. He knew he wanted some of what he had to offer.

Once the party was coming to an end, Calvin walked his girlfriend to her car. He came back inside and began saying his goodbyes to everyone who was sober enough to leave. Christopher knew it was now or never.

He approached Calvin and asked him if he could talk to him upstairs. Calvin seemed intrigued and told him to meet him in the pool house out back instead.

Christopher went first, and about five minutes later, Calvin came inside behind him. Chris took a deep breath and just blurted everything out.

"I've been thinking about you ever since I saw you at the coffee house. I don't want to offend you, and I know you have a girlfriend, but I can't help but feel there is something between us."

Calvin walked over to Chris who was preparing to be punched or something worse. Instead, he gave him a long, deep, passionate kiss. His lips tasted of Hennessy. Calvin reached down and grabbed Christopher's firm round bottom. He felt himself grow harder from the embrace.

When they managed to come up for air, Calvin explained how he felt the same attraction too. He always had sexual feelings towards men but liked women too· He was too scared and confused to act on his desires, that was until he

met Christopher.

They began kissing as Christopher took off his pants.

Calvin grabbed his penis and began stroking it slowly. He

licked the palm of his hand and rubbed Chris's pipe again.

It was rock hard and ready for anything.

Christopher yanked off Calvin's joggers and exposed his

huge shaft. It was fully engorged and ready to go. Chris got

on his knees and began showing Calvin just how much he

wanted him. Calvin's legs shook so hard he almost lost his

balance. They decided to take their talents into the

bedroom, grabbing their clothes, and locked the door

behind them. Christopher pushed Calvin to the bed and

took him back into his mouth. He sucked and licked like a

professional and had Calvin squirting in his mouth in no

time. He licked Calvin's ass and stuck a finger inside of

him. He stimulated his G-spot and had Calvin moaning in ecstasy.

Next, Calvin went to the dresser and grabbed the Vaseline. Chris laughed and told him there was no need. He explained that the butthole gets as wet as a vagina and that he could slide it on it. He walked him through putting it in slowly, but Calvin was a natural.

Before they knew it, Calvin was beating up Chris' hole like a pussy. Chris was so wet and tight, way different than anything Calvin had ever felt. They were kissing and licking all over each other. It was rough and sensual all at the same time. Chris came first and Calvin shortly after. They laid in bed and cuddled all night long.

Around six in the morning, they were awakened to Calvin's phone ringing. It was Delilah, his girlfriend. The look of fear came over his face followed by a smile. He hit ignore and kissed Christopher instead. He would have to figure out life eventually, but for now, all he wanted was to be inside Chris again. He finally got a taste of what he'd been desiring and wasn't about to stop now.

Swingers Soirée

Jackie and Ron were the epitome of the middle class. They had the two children, dog, and house with the white picket fence. Ron owned a used car dealership and Jackie was a high school principal at a charter school. They had been married for fifteen years and were truly each other's better half.

They had a decent sex life for a normal couple married for that long, but it wasn't enough. They longed for the ability to get wild and crazy and settled on the art of swinging. They did a lot of research and joined a swingers group on social media.

In the beginning, they often just went inside the group to look around and would seldom participate in discussions. After a few months had passed they warmed up and were active members. They were invited to the group's next event and decided they'd give it a go.

Jackie was especially nervous. She was a forty-something-year-old mom and a high school principal. What if one of the parents was at the party and recognized her? Plus, she wasn't as in shape as she used to be in her prime. She decided a nice flowing wrap dress would suit her figure and be perfect for the occasion.

Ron, on the other hand, was elated. He chose a nice Polo shirt and dark washed jeans. He packed their swimsuits, because they were told the pool would be open and heated. They dropped their kids off to their aunts' and headed two hours away to the secret location.

They pulled up to a mansion with a steel gate. Everything looked so modern and expensive. They were asked the secret password through telecom and were buzzed right in. They parked their car, grabbed each other's hand and walked inside.

It looked like the scene out of a movie. There were drinks and appetizers being passed out by the waitstaff. There were people in regular clothes mingling with naked or close to naked people. They decided to walk around and take a tour of the fabulous place.

The floors were a beautiful white marble all throughout the mansion. Floor to ceiling windows and everything run by technology. Each room they looked in seemed to have a random couple or few getting it on. They saw a girl on girl, girl on guy, a guy on guy, and orgies galore. Outside of each room was a table full of condoms and sexual enhancers. It was a lot to take in and they felt mutually overwhelmed.

They decided to just get a few drinks in their systems and go for a swim. They downed enough liquor to knock the edge off and changed into their bathing suits.

Inside the pool was a couple making out and a three-way going on in the hot tub. They climbed inside and began rubbing on each other. That liquor must have done the trick because they were ready to have a little fun. They gravitated towards another shy-looking couple on the other side of the pool. They decided to make a conversation and hit it off immediately. Their names were Armando and Aisha. They were thirty-something and married and looking to spice up their love life as well.

After they felt they were comfortable enough, they decided to find an empty room to get better acquainted. They grabbed another tray of drinks and settled on a room with a massive California king-size bed. They sipped, smoked a little pot, and laughed.

Once they were good and buzzed they decided to play a rousing game of truth or dare. Ron went first. Armando, the other husband, dared Ron to kiss Aisha. It was the first woman he'd kissed other than his wife in years and he was nervous. Jackie rubbed his back and told him it was ok. She was just as eager to see the two make out. She didn't know what had gotten inside of her, but all her inhibitions were gone and she was a woman on the prowl.

He walked up to Aisha and gave her a passionate but quick kiss. She blushed and complimented him on his technique. Next, it was Jackie's turn and she was dared to kiss Armando. He was a Middle Eastern man with urban swag. He grabbed her by the back of her head and tongued her down something proper. She had never been kissed like that before and could see why Aisha snatched him right up.

Next, Aisha was dared to take off her bikini top. She had perky breasts and nipples. Her areoles were large and hard. Jackie wanted to taste them so she leaned over and took one into her mouth.

That must've been the exact thing needed to really kick it up a notch because before they knew it everyone was all over everyone. Aisha was making out with Ron. Armando was licking on Jackie's neck and make his way to her pussy. Aisha made her way down to Ron's penis. Jackie and Ron held hands as they were orally pleased into ecstasy. They even seemed to cum at the exact same moment.

Next, Aisha laid back and Jackie decided to get a taste of her. She was trimmed down neatly and smelled of coconut oil. She tasted even better than she smelled. She licked all around and even penetrated her with her tongue. The men stood and watched as the performance reached a climactic ending. They were both jacking off from the sight of it all.

Armando was the more dominant male and decided to slide inside of Jackie. Her ass was up in the air while eating at the perfect angle for him to get deep inside. He thrust with such force and it felt so good. He was bigger than Ron and thicker too. She moaned load and was dripping wet. Ron decided he'd let Jackie enjoy her pleasure, and took over eating out Aisha. He worked his tongue all around and right and she was ready to cum he slid himself deep inside of her. She squirted all over him and he was turned on

Jackie told him to "bring his dick here," and sucked all of Aisha's juices off of him. He was so hard he went back inside Aisha and beat her pussy as he'd never stroked before.

The sight of it all made Armando so excited he came all inside of Jackie. Ron came inside of Aisha shortly after. They laid in the bed, all four of them, in complete silence. All you could hear was their heavy breathing from the marathon session they just had.

They decided to exchange numbers and friended each other on Facebook. This was the most fun and excitement any of them had ever had. They were officially part of the swinging lifestyle and the possibilities were endless.

Conclusion

I wrote this book to stimulate your mind and body. My words entered you and made itself at home.

My thoughts touched you in places that may have never been touched and I enjoyed every bit of it.

If you are sitting here; hot, bothered, and ready to act out your wildest fantasies, then my job is done.

Don't let another opportunity to pass you by to let it all go... put it all on the line and try "Something New". We only get one life, so you might as well live it to the fullest!

What are you afraid of?